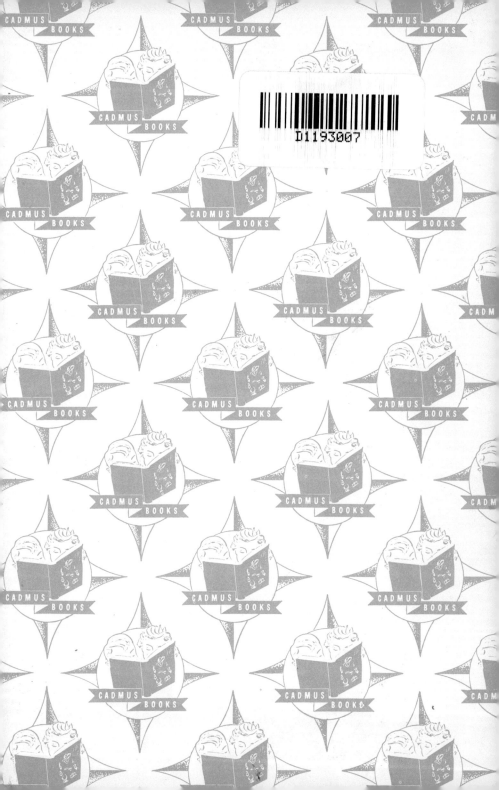

That Jud!

THAT JUD!

By ELSPETH BRAGDON
Illustrated by GEORGES SCHREIBER

The Maine orphan was always referred to as "that Jud", sometimes with great affection by the man he lived with, a retired sea-captain, and Father Tom and Mr. York, who believed in him, but with great exasperation by others, like the housekeeper. "That Jud" was lonely and built a cabin on a nearby island, just to have something of his own. But when there was a crisis in the village, he was blamed instead of praised, as he should have been. He earned his own self-respect, as well as that of the townspeople.

* * * *

Dewey Decimal Classification: Fic

That Jud!

BY ELSPETH BRAGDON
Illustrated by Georges Schreiber

1962 FIRST CADMUS EDITION
THIS SPECIAL EDITION IS PUBLISHED BY ARRANGEMENT WITH
THE PUBLISHERS OF THE REGULAR EDITION
THE VIKING PRESS, INC.
BY
E. M. HALE AND COMPANY
EAU CLAIRE, WISCONSIN

Dedicated to
Captain Archie S. Spurling
of Islesford, Maine
1861—1950

✓

I am grateful to the editors of *The Maine Coast Fisherman* for permission to use Gordon W. Thomas's exciting story about the wreck of the schooner *Yosemite*.

Contents

1. Jud of Spruce Point, Maine   11

2. Miz Hanks Speaks Her Mind   21

3. Homer Lends a Hand   31

4. Everything Goes Wrong   39

5. There's No Harm in Asking   49

6. Jud Gets a Job, and Does a Job   59

7. Someone New in Town   65

8. The Wonderful Week   75

9. Jud Sees His Stove   81

10. Fire!   87

11. Father Tom and Captain Ben Stand By   97

12. Maybe—Perhaps—Do You Suppose?   113

13. This Way, It's Just Right   121

That Jud!

1. Jud of Spruce Point, Maine

I F YOU could, for only part of a day, be a seagull wheeling and swooping over a green-spiked spur of land known as Spruce Point, Maine, you would see many things. You would see, first of all, the blue sky with great puffs of windy clouds boiling up out of the north. You would see the far horizon where the sky and ocean meet. In the harbor you would see the small boats of lobstermen and the draggers used by fishermen and a dozen or more skiffs and dories tied up at a small dock. On the dock, probably five or six old men would sit, silently smoking, watching the younger men dumping lobsters into the pound or taking them out to weigh for somebody's supper.

Seagulls find their food in the ocean or around docks, but they are not too proud to patrol the land too, so you would see women at their kitchen doors and children in the schoolyard and old Mrs. Gilley sweeping off the porch of her store and Captain Ben painting the picket fence in front of his house with slow careful strokes. Down Sandy Road, where the boathouses are, you would see a young man working on the motor of a boat hauled up on the shore.

All this you would see, but you would hear little, for seagulls are almost the noisiest birds in the world. They screech and whine so loudly that they must be surprised when a really big noise drowns out their own racket.

However, if you, as a person, listened, you would hear everyone in the village of Spruce Point, Maine, say at least once every day the same thing. Everyone said, with a shake of the head, "That Jud!"

The old men on the dock, noticing a dory badly tied, with an oarlock and oar left on the gunwale, shook their heads and said, "That Jud!"

The woman at her kitchen door, seeing the prints of running feet in her flower garden, said crossly, "That Jud!"

The children on the swings outside the school, seeing a basketball fly clean and sure through the hoop nailed to the big maple tree, said admiringly, "That Jud!"

Old Mrs. Gilley, finding a basket of wild raspberries tucked behind her porch post, said it lovingly.

The men in the boathouses, not being able to put their hands quickly to a chisel or hammer, said it angrily.

The young man working on the motor down on the shore straightened up and stretched. Then he grinned as if he had remembered something very funny. "That Jud!" he said.

About the only person in the whole village who was

never heard to say anything—lovingly, admiringly, or crossly—about Jud Lurvey, twelve years old, was Captain Ben. That was strange, for Jud lived with the old man, and you might think Captain Ben would have the most to say. But Captain Ben wasn't much of a talker—that is, not about people. He watched them. He did a lot of quiet figuring about them. But he didn't say much. He had spent most of his life on the big coastwise schooners of long ago. He had come home to stay, and he had plenty to think about. If you should ask him right out what he thought about Jud, or ask,

as one irritated old neighbor once did, "Ain't that Jud an awful trial to you?" he'd look you over quietly for a long minute. Then he'd turn slowly on the heel of his polished shoe and walk away, his back very straight and his head very high. No, Captain Ben wasn't much of a talker.

At half-past one on a mild May day, three old men sat in the lee of the dock shed, soaking up sunshine and pulling on their pipes. They had known each other for seventy years, more or less, and, as Captain Lu said, they had "about run out of talk." In silence they took note of wind and weather; in silence they watched the activity on the dock, sitting up a little straighter when a strange boat came into the harbor and observing its conduct with experienced and critical eyes.

Now Captain Lu took his pipe from his mouth and pointed with its stem to a dory drifting down the wind toward the mouth of the harbor. "Ain't that Ben's boy?" he asked. "Shouldn't he be up to the schoolhouse this time of day?"

" 'Tain't much after one o'clock," said Captain Fred. "The whistle over to Hardwick at the fish factory just blew. Maybe it's some kind of holiday."

Captain Lu smiled. "It's a holiday that Jud thought up if it's any holiday at all," he said. "He'll get it when Ben finds out he's skipped school. Ben thinks a lot of schooling. Always did."

Jud couldn't, of course, hear what the old captains said, nor would he have cared much if he had heard. He sat half slumped over his drawn-in oars, feeling the wind blow through his short red hair and the sun warm on his back and legs, bare below the rolled-up blue jeans. He listened to the soft slap of waves against the dory and the whiny cry of seagulls overhead. In the bow of the dory a small, rough-haired dog half stood, half squatted, his forepaws on the gunwale. He was, Jud would tell you, "a sort of terrier," and went by the proud name of Skipper. He was as at home in boats as he was ashore, and now his ears, one black, one white, were cocked high, and his small black-tipped nose quivered with excitement.

"Pretty," Jud said aloud to Skipper, who barked once sharply in reply. "Real pretty day." His glance rested briefly on the dock, and from there followed the winding road that led up to the schoolhouse. Its neat yellow walls and wide windows caught the sun and held it.

"Phooey," said Jud. "Phooey to school!"

In his mind's eye he could see the big room, geraniums in the window, Mrs. Crockett, his teacher, looking over her glasses at the rows and rows of—here Jud's mouth straightened into a thin line of disgust—*girls!* What kind of school was it where there was just one boy? Jud's gaze fled from the schoolhouse, and he noticed suddenly that the dory was moving swiftly along the rocky shore in the ebbing tide. He seized the oars and pulled on them.

"Gol*lee!*" he cried. "I mighta missed it!"

"It" was Nubbin Island, lying just at the mouth of the harbor—an island so small that it seemed to float on the water like a shell carrying a few little pine trees under which some coarse spiny grass grew in a halfhearted sort of way. Jud pulled on the starboard oar hard and nosed the dory up to flattish rock across which a low branch of pine reached. Before the boat touched the shore Skipper leaped out and dashed up the rocks, exploring as if this were not a second home to him.

Pulling in the oars and grabbing the painter, Jud scrambled out of the boat and tied it to the low branch. He looked around him, a wide grin of happiness on his face. "Good old Nubbin!" he said to the small island approvingly.

Then he pushed his way between the interlacing branches of the four trees, which were not much taller than he. Within the circle of trees a large piece of old sailcloth covered a strange-looking object, and Jud's first action was to remove the rocks that held the

sailcloth down at each corner. Pushing the sailcloth back, he squatted on his heels and took stock of what had been hidden so carefully.

"There's 'most enough boards for the sides," he said in a figuring sort of way. "Sides and either a roof or a floor. Can't have both for awhile." He sat and considered, poking his brown fingers into the coarse grass under the trees.

"Not enough dirt here, or grass either, to hold water when it rains," he decided. "It'll run right off, most of it. And the sun will dry the earth quickly after the rain's over. I won't need a floor right off. I'll have a roof."

He leaned forward and poked at the pile of boards. "It's safe—my window frame—my perfectly good

window frame. And only one light busted!" The boy stood up slowly and pushed back the branches of one of the trees that hid the view of the open sea, with the surf breaking far out over Old Fiddleback Ledge.

"I'll chop these branches out," he said. "I'll set my camp so the window will give right on the open place. Then I'll sit inside and watch things, and, unless they look hard, no one will see me at all." He pulled Skipper to him and hugged the wriggling little dog close. "It will be our house," he said, "our very own house!"

With a yip, Skipper broke away from him and dashed to the edge of the rocks. Jud went on inspecting his pile of boards and driftwood.

"I oughta have a stove," he said slowly, "an old piece of stovepipe and a stove." His thin face looked very determined. "I'll find one," he went on. "And when I've built our camp, maybe they'll call this 'Jud's Island.' It will look good on the charts—'Jud's Island.' "

His face crinkled into a slow smile as he carefully replaced the canvas and snugged it down around his lumber pile. If it weren't for school and chores, there'd be time to build the camp quickly, before summer came. With the coming of summer, the small harbor would be alive with the hurrying business of lobstering. It wouldn't be easy then to collect more wood or build anything without being noticed. Jud's mouth firmed into a straight line once more.

"School . . . phooey," he said again. Then he went

back to the dory, untied it, and pushed it out, jumping in lightly before the tide caught it. Skipper followed close upon his heels. Jud picked up the oars and swung the boat around. As he did so, he caught a glimpse of a gabled roof and four red chimneys that were a sort of landmark to all the boatmen of the area. They stood out between and above the small clustering pine trees on Easterly Point, directly across from Nubbin Island. Everyone knew that they belonged to Mr. York's place. Jud let the tide move his boat along gently and looked thoughtfully at the roof line above the trees.

Many harbors and small towns along the Maine coast have become big or small summer resorts to which people from near and far come, either to rent houses hastily vacated by "natives" or to build big sprawling houses near the water. Spruce Point was, however, almost unvisited by summer people. The roads leading to it were dusty and deeply rutted, so that low-slung cars scraped their bellies as they crawled slowly over the twenty miles from the nearest highway. And while the harbor was deep and well-protected, it was small, and crowded by the boats of fishermen and lobstermen.

But years ago, before Jud was born, Mr. York had come into the harbor in his big sloop, forced to give up his easterly cruise for a few days by a thick fog and cold rain. He had come ashore with his young wife, and, because he was a friendly sort of person, had made himself liked. In turn, he had liked the people of the village. When the fog lifted and he had set out again, he had called out to the men on the dock, "We'll be back next summer. Watch out for us!"

Sure enough, he did come back the next July, and before he left he had bought the land on Easterly Point. During the next winter the village men were glad of the work he gave them building the house on the rocks.

Jud eyed it now consideringly. There was the big house, and a small house for guests, he knew. There were a garage and two sheds for storage. Everyone in the village knew that Mr. York had a liking for what many of them called "junk": old chairs, maybe with a rung broken or a worn-out rush seat; tables, scarred and battered by long use but still firm on their legs; and—here Jud whistled sharply—stoves, especially Franklin stoves, those wonderful squat little stoves that heated a room far better than a fireplace, with neat folding doors that opened to show the fire or closed to force a draft. Mr. York was crazy about stoves.

I bet, Jud said to himself, I bet— And he turned the boat with a strong pull on one oar and headed it in to Easterly Point.

2. Miz Hanks Speaks Her Mind

JUD scuffed his way up the powdery dirt road that led from the dock, with no heart in him for whistling. Skipper had deserted him to go up the road as fast as he could toward the supper he hoped would be waiting for him. The old captains were gone from their bench, as were the younger men from the lobster pound. All the boats were tied at their moorings, riding quietly on the pale, still sea across which the light slanted narrowly.

These signs meant that Jud would be late for supper and that Miz Hanks, who kept house for Captain Ben, would be mad. What's more, it hadn't been worth risking her bawling-out to poke around Mr. York's place. Everything had been tight as a drum, with tar-paper nailed fast over the narrow windows of the shed.

There had been one door with a hasp he could have pried off, but he had long ago decided that while it was all right to pick up things folks didn't want, it was wrong to break in and take things. Break in and carry stuff off—oh no, not for Jud!

So, in disappointment and mild dread of Miz Hanks' sharp tongue, Jud scrunched his shoulders together and went more and more slowly along the road. Ladder Moore, so called for his gangling height and his way of leaning against anything handy, hailed him as he passed the general store. Ladder, as everyone knew, wasn't very bright, but he was friendly enough.

"Hi!" called Ladder. "Hear you skipped school today. Guess you'll get a licking this time." And he laughed his silly, high-pitched laugh, eying Jud with a sly, pleased look. He didn't mean any harm. He was, for all his age and man's size, a small boy trying to act smart. So there wasn't any point in answering back or getting mad, Jud knew. The boy could feel his face getting red, however, and he hurried a little.

The side door of the store opened, and old Mrs. Gilley stood there, balancing a pile of empty cartons. "Set these down for me, Jud, will you?" she asked pleasantly.

Jud took the cartons to the pile, which would be burned after the next rain. When he came back, Mrs. Gilley looked at him rather unhappily. "Why did you do it, Jud?" she asked kindly. "Why'd you skip school? Weren't you feeling good?"

Jud liked Mrs. Gilley, and if Ladder hadn't been near enough to hear everything he might have told her how he hated being the only boy, and how restless he felt, anyway, by the time May came around. But as it was, he said nothing, just shrugged his shoulders and started home again.

Captain Ben's house was small and white, as neat and handy inside as a ship. Even the picket fence and small flower garden were tidy, and the back door in the kitchen ell which Jud entered was freshly painted. Captain Ben sat in his rocker by the stove, reading the Bangor paper, and he only glanced briefly at Jud over the top of his glasses.

Miz Hanks was scrubbing the last of the pots and pans at the sink. When she heard the door close behind Jud, she turned on her heel and faced him, wiping her hands angrily. She was a tall, thin, knobby kind of woman, and right now her black eyes fairly snapped.

"This is a fine time of night to come strammin' in here!" she snapped. "Maybe you think I'm running a hotel, meals served to order at all hours, day and night," she continued with fine sarcasm.

Jud said nothing. He slid into a chair by the door and let the high-pitched voice run over him like a wave. Skipper, who had been licking up the last bits on his plate, came to stand beside the quiet boy.

"What you got to say for yourself?" Miz Hanks went on. "It's all over town you skipped school, so don't think

you're fooling anyone. Ain't you 'shamed of yourself? Can't you say you're sorry?"

Jud shook his head. "I'm not sorry," he said slowly.

Miz Hanks crossed the kitchen quickly and took his shoulder between her thin fingers. "Well, you *ought* to be sorry and 'shamed," she said. "How many boys have a good home like yours, where folks are willing for you to go to school instead of getting out to earn your keep, the way lots of twelve-year-old boys do?"

As Jud made no answer, she continued, "Do you call this being grateful for what this town—not to mention Captain Ben and me—does for you? After your pa was drowned and your ma died of the flu, what would have happened to you if the town hadn't taken care of you?" she asked, her voice hard and cross-sounding.

Jud stood up quickly, his hands clenched tight, and Skipper made the grumbling sound deep in his throat that passed for a growl.

Captain Ben threw down his paper and stood up with surprising speed. "We'll have none of that in this house," he said to Miz Hanks in the thundery kind of voice he'd used at sea. "You've gone too far, ma'am. This is Jud's home, same as it's mine."

Miz Hanks took her hand from Jud's shoulder and went back to the sink, sniffling a little.

Captain Ben stood in front of Jud, looking at him in silence for a long moment. Then he went back to his chair and picked up his paper. "I don't think much of skipping school," he said in a mild voice, as if he were talking to the newspaper. "Maybe it'll help you remember that I don't think much of it if you skip supper tonight. Wouldn't do you a mite of harm to go to bed early." The he began to read the paper in earnest.

Jud waited a minute. Miz Hanks would have to have the last word, he knew. When it came, it was surprisingly mild.

"You wash up good," she said. "Don't go wiping the dirt off on your towel."

Jud's room was over the kitchen ell, and his bed stood under the window at one end. After he had washed, Jud went over to the bed and knelt on it so that he could look down the road to the harbor. Skipper jumped lightly onto the bed—strictly against Miz Hanks' rules— and lay flat, his nose resting on the window ledge.

Lights were lit in every house now, and darkness was coming fast. Two little girls were playing hopscotch in the yard of the schoolhouse. Mrs. Crockett, who boarded down the road, was shutting up the school, a pile of books and papers hugged under her arm. She said something to the little girls, who screamed with laughter. Then they stopped their game and walked down the road with her. As they passed the general store Mrs. Gilley and Ladder Moore's mother called to the teacher, and she stopped to talk.

"Talking about me," said Jud. "Talking about how much it costs the town to board me with Captain Ben.

Saying I'm not thankful. Saying I skipped school. Well, I did. And I'll skip it again. I'm going to build my camp on the island, and I'll never go to school. I'll get right out of this town and I'll take care of myself. Nobody'll have to take care of me."

This was one of Jud's favorite plans, and it usually gave him great comfort. But tonight it didn't help much. Getting the camp built seemed a long way off. He'd have to have a stove. He'd have to buy things, and he never had more than a quarter at a time. Besides, he was awfully hungry. He pulled his knees up to his chin to hug the crawling ache out of his stomach. If he hadn't been twelve years old, he would have cried. As it was, there was a big lump in his throat that he couldn't seem to swallow. He put his head down on Skipper's rough coat. The little dog wriggled about until he could lick the boy's ear gently.

"I hate this town," Jud said out loud. "We'll run away, Skipper, the very first chance we get."

Suddenly Jud realized that there was a light coming up the stairs, and in a minute Captain Ben stood at the door, a kerosene lamp in one hand and a good-sized bowl in the other. Had he heard what the boy said about running away? If so, he showed no sign of it, but put the lamp down on the bureau. Then he sat down on one of the two straight chairs in the room, holding the bowl carefully.

"Ain't undressed yet, are you?" he asked pleasantly.

"Whyn't you get at it while I've got the light up here? Then you might like a mess of Indian pudding I found out in the cold closet." He didn't look at Jud, who began to untie his sneakers and pull off his T-shirt and jeans.

Captain Ben stirred the pudding cautiously. "She's a mite stingy with cream, but she's real lavish with raisins," he said. Then he looked at Jud and smiled. "I found a little jug of cream to go on top, and threw a handful of brown sugar on top of that." He handed the bowl to Jud, who began to spoon up the rich, sweet pudding eagerly.

The old man put his hand lightly on Skipper's head. "Better hop down, Skipper," he said. "Give the boy a mite more room." The little dog got down obediently and settled himself beside the bed.

When the pudding was all gone, Captain Ben took the bowl and set it on the chest of drawers beside the lamp. "Get in, boy," he said gently.

Jud got into bed, his stomach pleasantly full and the bedclothes comfortingly warm. The old man lit his pipe and leaned back, stretching his legs out long in front of him and looking about.

"Planned this house a good deal like a ship," he said. "This room's more like a ship's cabin than you'd think." He looked at the rounded planks of the ceiling and the cupboards built in under the eaves. "Always meant to build a bunk up here someday." Then he fell silent, blowing big puffs of smoke, which drifted across the room.

Slowly, as if he were remembering more than he could put into words, Captain Ben went on, "I wasn't any older than you when I shipped out on my first vessel. Out of Boothbay Harbor, it was, and her name was the *Abbie M. Deering.* She was the pride of the seiners, a hundred and three feet long, and her main boom was twice as long as this house. She was just covered with canvas, and an awful pretty sight." There was another long silence while Captain Ben smoked and Jud lay with half-closed eyes, picturing the big schooner like a great bird, its sails puffed out by the north wind.

"Her master," said Captain Ben, "was Captain John Seavey. He was a killer."

Jud opened his eyes wide and stared at the old man.

"He didn't *kill* anyone," Captain Ben said hastily, "but he was a hard master. He near worked us to death. The longest two years I ever spent before the mast were the two I spent with him. I was hungry and lonesome and dog tired the whole 'during time."

Captain Ben rose and picked up the lamp and bowl. He turned to the door. "Guess I didn't mention it," he said, not looking at Jud, "but I *ran away* to ship on that boat. Yessir, that was the only time in my life I ever ran away from anything."

Then he was gone, and the light went down the stairs with him. Jud jumped out of bed and ran to the door.

"Thank you, Captain Ben!" he shouted. "Thank you for the pudding."

Captain Ben turned on his heel and glared at him. "You *idjit!*" he roared. "Now she'll light into *me!*"

Jud jumped into bed, laughing to himself, and, in the middle of the laughter, fell asleep.

3. Homer Lends a Hand

THE last two weeks of the school year went pretty well, Jud thought. To be sure, the day after he skipped school he had to write two hundred times, "I will go to school and learn my lessons," but there could have been worse punishments. On the last day there had been a play at school, an annual affair which usually filled Jud's heart with dread and horror.

"Acting," he muttered. "Acting—with a mess of girls!"

But this year he had not been asked to take an acting part. Instead he had been named stage manager, importantly enough. The fairy coach that he made out of old cartons had looked so much like the coach in the pictures of Queen Elizabeth II's coronation that Mrs. Crockett was delighted.

"Isn't Jud smart!" she had said when the play was over. "Didn't he make a wonderful coach?"

Everyone had admired the coach—unless, of course, you counted Ladder, who asked in a sneery kind of voice where Jud had swiped the cartons. If Jud hadn't run angrily out of the hall, his pride hurt and his fun quite spoiled, he would have heard Mrs. Gilley's quick defense of him and Mrs. Crockett's statement that "there aren't any smarter, nicer boys than Jud anywhere—when he wants to be."

By the time school ended, daylight-saving time had come, which meant longer days for the camp that Jud had been planning all winter long. Now the camp really began to take shape. Captain Ben had asked no questions when the boy borrowed a "second-best" saw, an old hammer, and a box of used nails. Every morning the old dory, the boy, and Skipper could be seen heading along the shore for Nubbin Island.

Making the clearing in the handful of trees had not been too difficult, and when Jud laid out his lumber for the walls he could see there was going to be enough. But the first spell of bad weather showed him that he would have a damp cold floor, even if the ground was so thinly covered with soil. There was enough soil to hold the run-off of rain in an enclosed place where sun and wind would be slow to dry it out. There wasn't another piece of planking on the shore or in the village, Jud knew. He looked hungrily at the small brown building called "the old schoolhouse," now standing empty and unused. But it was still village property, and there would be trouble if Jud started pulling boards from its sides.

So one fine morning in June, instead of heading for Nubbin, Jud rowed from the dock in a southwesterly direction, toward the boathouses. The shore there was

pebbly, making a rough sort of beach, and it ought not
to be too hard to pick up enough rocks to cover the floor
space of his house.

As he came to the last boathouse he could hear a great
banging and thumping. Through the wide open door he
saw Homer, the best lobsterman in the village, working
hard on the engine of his boat, which was pulled up on
the ways.

Jud shouted, "Hi!" but the noise of hammering
drowned out his voice. So he pulled the dory up on
shore and began to fill it with flat rocks. The job was
made no easier by Skipper, who raced up and down the
shore crazily, barking at seagulls and chasing waves.
Two or three times the little dog got thoroughly
drenched, and, of course, waited until he was close to
Jud to shake himself thoroughly.

It was hard work, and the boy could see that it would
take a long time to gather one rock at a time and lug it
along the shore to the boat. What he needed was a basket, a bushel basket with handles. He went up to the
boathouse.

Homer had stopped hammering and was wiping the
sweat from his face and neck. The tall man saw Jud and
grinned at him. "Hi, Jud," he said amiably. "No school
today, huh?"

Jud felt that school was still a pretty sore point, and,
though he made no answer, he could feel his face
getting red.

Homer laughed and clapped him on the shoulder. "Forget it!" he shouted. "Don't let it get you down. Everybody skipped school once in their lives and got talked about too. Ever hear anybody tell tales about me when I was your age?"

Jud shook his head silently.

Homer's face looked angry for a moment. "Well, they did," he said slowly. "I guess they still do at times. Forget it," he repeated. "Pretty soon you'll be old enough to get out of here and go to a bigger place."

Jud looked along the shore. The sky was bright and clear over the fresh green of the meadow; the small village houses and the church, neatly painted white, were pretty as a picture. And the sea was a deep blue,

curling over on itself, and ruffled along its edge with
white. Go away from here? He shook his head.

Then he looked around the boat shed. "Got a basket?"
he asked eagerly. "I'm getting some rocks, and it's an
awful slow, tedious job, carrying them one by one."

Homer eyed him curiously. "Getting rocks, eh?" he
asked. "Making something, maybe?"

Jud didn't answer, but Homer went on, as if he didn't
expect an answer. "I had me a cave once," he said,
squatting on his heels and lighting a cigarette. "Over
on the shore where York bought, it was. You had to get
down on all fours to get in the opening, but once you
were inside you could stand up. I rigged an old tarpau-
lin over the door, and it was good and snug inside.

Never could figure out a chimney, though. When I built me a fire in there I darn near suffocated. But it was mine," he said quietly.

Jud forgot about his secret for a moment. "That's it!" he cried, his eyes shining with excitement. "You've got to have something all yours, just the way you want it." He paused. "Was the floor of your cave good and dry?"

Homer shook his head. "Not in rainy spells, it wasn't," he said. "You'd think that if there was no place for the smoke to go out there'd be no place for the rain to come in. But it did. I had to make a kind of drainage ditch along one wall for the water to run off." He grinned. "I didn't have to lug rocks for a floor," he added.

Jud stood very still for a moment, looking at the tall young man with the big grin. Then he grinned too. "I got me the makings of a camp," the boy said softly. "It's going to be on Nubbin. It's a secret; but you can see it if you want. It's going to be *neat*, real neat."

Homer put his tools up on a shelf and looked at his boat. "Can't do much more till the mail comes in, with the parts I ordered from Hardwick," he said. "Two hours, I've got. Come on, boy, let's get going."

That was the beginning of a real fine time. From the first, Homer seemed to see just how the camp would be, even when it was nothing but a cleared place in a clump of trees and a pile of old boards. Even when his engine was fixed and he went back to his daily tour of lobster traps, he'd stop at Nubbin for an hour before

supper. He and Jud would hammer, saw, and nail side
by side. Everything went together quickly and neatly
with two working at it. Almost in no time the little camp
stood solidly between the trees, looking out to sea, its
one-pitch roof tight against the weather, and the stone
floor smoothly laid, with a drain-off ditch at each side.
Homer had provided an old door and the glass for the
one broken window light.

At last it was done, and the two sat on the rocks in
front of the camp, feeling well pleased. Jud was so
happy he could hardly speak. Finally he cleared his
throat. "We'd oughta celebrate, sort of," he said gruffly.

"Fire off a cannon, maybe?" Homer laughed.

Jud frowned a little. This was no joke to him. "We
can't celebrate here," he said slowly. "You're the only
one who knows about my camp, and that's the way I
want it to be. If we let off steam in the village, someone would find out why for sure."

It was Homer's turn to be silent. He had heard every
man in the village speak about the camp during the
last week. They had seen it as they went out in their
boats, and anyone within three miles could have heard
the hammering that had gone on. They had had secrets
too, when they were boys. There wasn't one of them,
no matter how openly critical or complaining he might
be about Jud at times, who would spoil Jud's fun by
letting on that he knew. Most of them liked him better
for having had the idea and the spunk to carry it out.

"Tell you what," Homer said thoughtfully. "Tomorrow's Friday, when the stores up to Hardwick stay open until nine o'clock. We could go over there in my truck right after supper, and after I do a couple of errands we could go to a show. How'd that be?"

Jud beamed with pleasure. He grinned so widely that it almost hurt. He held out his hand to Homer. "Shake on it," he said.

4. Everything Goes Wrong

BY FIVE o'clock the next day, Jud was the most excited person in the village. He had had a bath in the big washtub out in the shed ell, and had put on clean blue jeans and a bright-patterned shirt that he kept for best. Captain Ben, entering into the spirit of the thing, had given the boy a lick-and-a-promise haircut, so the cowlick on the crown of his head no longer waved on high like a red flag. Jud fed Skipper and shut him up in his room, explaining carefully that he was going to a show in Hardwick.

When they sat down to an early supper of creamed codfish and baked potatoes, Miz Hanks glanced at the boy with an approving look that was as rare as it was pleasant. "I declare," she said, spooning the thick, smooth fish sauce onto her potato, "you look almost civilized! Now see that you behave yourself when you get to the picture show."

Jud nodded, trying to eat his supper but not feeling hungry at all.

"That's right," Captain Ben said slowly. "You're going to the show. Who's going to pay?"

Jud put down his fork. He'd never thought about that. When Homer had said, "Let's go to the show," it didn't sound like money at all. It sounded free, sort of, though Jud knew perfectly well that on Friday night the show cost forty cents. Now his heart sank. He couldn't let Homer pay, after all the work he had done on the camp.

Captain Ben was watching him quietly. Then he put his hand in his waistcoat pocket, the small one, against which his gold watch chain lay snugly. He took out something folded up into a small wad and slid it along the clean tablecloth. "Here's in case you're a little short of cash," he said gruffly.

Jud unfolded the square. It was a dollar bill, more money than he had ever had at one time before. It was enough for two tickets to the show and two bags of popcorn. What could he ever say in thanks for this wonderful and unexpected gift? He gulped hard.

"Say thank you," Miz Hanks snapped. "And put it away careful, where you won't lose it."

A car horn blatted three times, outside and Jud jumped up. He stuffed the bill into his shirt pocket and started for the door. Then he stopped and came back slowly to the old man. "Thanks a lot," he said gruffly. Then he ran out, slamming the door after him, half hearing Miz Hanks' reproving cry, and headed for the cab of the truck.

He had one foot on the step before Homer spoke.

"Guess you'd better ride in back," he said. "Dianne here's got a real fancy dress on, and it would get squashed with three of us up here."

Jud stepped back and for a long minute stared up into the cab. There, sitting real close to Homer, was Dianne Bryant, her hair all curled up and lipstick on. For a moment he wanted to stay home. How could Homer have asked a girl to go on their private celebration?

Then Homer raced the motor and shouted above the roar, "Get in, kid, time's a-wastin'!" and before Jud knew it he was sitting on a box in the back of the truck, hanging on tightly as it bounced over the hard, rutty road to Hardwick. He could hear Homer and that girl laughing and singing up front, and he wished again he had never come. Then he had a sudden idea. Probably Dianne wanted to go shopping in Hardwick; she had *asked* to ride over. Lots of people did, all the time. Jud began to feel better. He put his hand in his shirt pocket and found the dollar bill. Everything was going to be all right. They'd get rid of that old girl and have a high old time at the show—popcorn and everything.

The Bijou Theater is at the east end of Hardwick and, as it was still early for the show, Jud was surprised when the truck drew up in front of the brightly lit entrance.

"I'll go along with you while you do the errands!" he shouted. "Then we'll come back for the show."

"Well, kid," Homer said slowly, "our plans are changed a little. Dianne and me are going over to the far side of town—dancing. You go on into the show. I'll give you the money. We'll pick you up afterward. How's that?"

Jud stood very still for a moment. Then he climbed down slowly from the truck. "I've got the money," he said proudly. "I've got money for the both of us and popcorn too."

Homer didn't meet his eyes, but raced the motor again. "We'll be seeing you!" he called. "Have fun!" And off the truck sped into Hardwick.

It was a long half-hour before the show opened, and by the time the cashier took her place at the ticket window Jud knew all the pictures in the entry by heart. It looked like a pretty good show, a Western, but Jud had no wish to see it. He was so full of disappointment, and of some kind of miserableness for which he had no name, that no show on earth seemed worth seeing. But he went in when the doors opened and found a seat way down front. First came the news and the sports pictures. Then came the advertisements— the Penney store, the Yellow and Brown Garage, and Bartlett's Drugstore. He knew them all by heart. Then, with a burst of trumpets, the feature picture began.

To this day, Jud couldn't tell you what it was about. All he could think of was that he'd have to ride home as he came, in the back of the truck, hearing the laughter and singing up front.

"I hate her," he whispered to himself. "If it hadn't been for her—" But he couldn't finish that sentence even to himself, for he knew from the way Homer hadn't been able to look him in the eyes that Dianne hadn't invited herself to come along, but had been asked, special.

I hate him, Jud thought. I'll never speak to him again as long as I live.

He was one of the last to leave the theater when the show was over, but there was no truck out front. He hung around until the cashier's window was empty and the lights went out. Golly, Homer was awful late. Maybe he wasn't coming. Maybe he'd even forgotten that Jud existed!

Cars had been going east past the Bijou every few minutes, and any one of them would probably have given him a lift. But by now traffic seemed to have stopped. The road to Spruce Point was empty and dark and, Jud knew, long. But he wasn't going to wait around all night for someone who didn't care what happened to him, so, turning up his coat collar, he set off down the road.

There was real chill in the night air, and a small wind blew steadily from the north, so Jud struck up as good a pace as he could keep to between the ruts. There was no moon, but the stars were bright. Walking fast was good for two things: it kept him warm and it helped the angry, hurt feeling in the pit of his stomach. He passed without a glance the gasoline station with its string of bright lights that marked the edge of Hardwick, his mind full of the spoiled celebration and of being forgotten at the end.

"I hate him," Jud muttered to himself. "If he came along right now, I wouldn't even get in his old truck."

When, after Jud had walked more than two miles, a fisherman from South Hardwick slowed down and offered

him a lift in his old car as far as the turn-off road, he
had nothing to say except a gruff "Thanks" when he got
out near the boathouses. The first one he came to was
Homer's, and he stood in the darkness, glaring at it.

"A fine friend you turned out to be!" he shouted at
the square black shape. "You didn't give a darn about
me if you could go dancing with that old girl. You
were glad to see the last of me when you set me down
at the show."

Then he leaned down and reached around him on

the ground. Straightening up, he let fly with the rock that had been so convenient to his hand, and was rewarded by the silvery crash of breaking glass. He found another stone and another, and he heaved them with all his strength at the small low windows. When he was done, he felt a little better, but more scared than anything else.

He squared his shoulders. "Good enough for you," he said, as if Homer were there.

As he went through the village he looked at the houses, most of them still and dark under the starry sky. There was a small dim light in the store, and around the corner he could see the light in Captain Ben's kitchen.

Oh no, he thought, he couldn't be sitting up for me. What will I say? He walked slowly up the path and opened the door quietly. The kitchen was empty. A note on the table was covered with Miz Hanks' sprawly handwriting. "Put out the light," he read. "Fix the latch on the kitchen door."

Moving as quietly as he could, Jud fastened the door and blew out the lamp. Then he climbed the stairs to his room. The hurt and anger filled him up as he remembered how excited he had been only a few hours ago. He pulled off his clothes and flung himself on the bed, burying his head in the pillow. Skipper jumped up and lay close to him.

"It wasn't fair," Jud whispered to Skipper. "I'm glad I broke his old windows. It wasn't fair at all." Then the

room was quiet. The village was quiet. There was no sound at all except the wind whining a little in the deep woods and the sea crashing softly on the rocky shore.

Then the silence was broken. Far down the road, a truck clattered and jounced. In a minute or two it had passed Captain Ben's, leaving behind it the sound of two people singing—two people, a man and a girl.

5. There's No Harm in Asking

IF THE next day hadn't been a special Saturday, Jud
would have been rousted out early by Miz Hanks.
But this, the third Saturday of the month, was the
day when half a dozen women from Spruce Point were
responsible for readying the "Congo" church in Hardwick for Sunday services. Early in the day they rode
over to the bigger town, filled with pride and impor-
tance. They took armfuls of fresh crisp flowers from their
gardens and plunged them into great crocks of cold
water to keep fresh; they dusted the pews and arranged
the hymnals; they rubbed the pulpit with wax and
polished it. Oh, there was plenty of work to keep Miz
Hanks away from home that day!

If, when Captain Ben had finished his six-o'clock
breakfast, he had not found the woodbox well filled and
a neat pile of wood cut to stove length outside the ell
door, he would have called Jud to do these daily chores.
As it was, after his breakfast and his first pipe of the
day Captain Ben went to the dock.

So, in the small room above the ell, with its ceiling
bowed over his head like that of a ship's cabin, Jud

slept late, the hurt forgotten. And because he slept, he missed one of the most pleasant events in the year for the people of Spruce Point. For in mid-morning the big white yawl belonging to Mr. York turned its bow into the channel between Nubbin and the shore, and, its sails neatly furled, moved steadily by its auxiliary motor, headed for its mooring. As Mr. York was one of the nicest people in the world, there was considerable excitement on the dock. The young men at the lobster pound shouted and waved. One of them set out in his dory to meet the yawl. The older men, Captain Ben among them, let their pipes go out as they watched the big boat come in. Most of them had spent most of their lives under sail, and, while the yawl was a "pleasure boat," she brought to mind memories of old days when they were young and life was an adventure in far places.

It took some little time to make the big boat fast and leave things shipshape before going ashore, but the men on the dock watched every familiar move with interest. When it was time for Mr. York and his wife to come ashore, he could be seen lifting a shiny object into the dinghy.

"Outboard motor," said Captain Lu approvingly. "Big bayster too."

They saw Mrs. York settle herself in the mid-seat of the dinghy, and in a moment Mr. York had cast off. The motor roared mightily and in less time than it takes to tell it the dinghy had crossed the gap of water and had pulled into the dock. Ladder Moore had brought his big wheelbarrow down to the dock as soon as the yawl was sighted, and he gathered up the bags, taking them over to the house on Easterly Point after everyone had greeted Mrs. York.

Mr. York, surrounded by an admiring group of men, held the new motor and pointed out its new improvements. Other men at the harbor had outboards, but none were as powerful or adaptable as this latest model.

Captain Ben eyed it respectfully. "Musta cost a pretty penny," he said.

Mr. York smiled. "Well, she's good enough to take care of," he agreed. "I want to keep her under cover here at the dock. I was thinking on the way here that I wish there were some young feller to take charge of the dinghy and motor, ferry us out to the yawl, run errands up to Hardwick—things like that. She's heavy, so I'd need someone with a strong back and arms. But it isn't hard to learn to run her."

Captain Ben looked thoughtful. "Guess you'll have to find someone at Hardwick," he said slowly. "Them as is strong enough are too busy with their own boats and traps this time of year."

Mr. York shook his head. "I don't want someone from Hardwick," he said firmly. "It wouldn't be hard work. A boy could do it. How about your boy, Captain Ben?"

A sudden silence fell. Ladder Moore, who, as the

villagers said, knew everything that happened and lots of things that didn't, had already told them of the broken windows at Homer's boathouse. No one had said, "That Jud!" but it had been in many minds. Only Captain Ben was sure that this could have been none of Jud's work, for he knew the boy thought a lot of Homer.

"He's kind of young," he said slowly. "We'll have to figure on it a bit."

·When the motor was stowed away and Mr. York had walked across the field to his house, the men at the dock returned to their usual activity. A few of the old men sat in the sun and watched, but Captain Ben walked slowly back to his house. When he went into the kitchen he found Jud at the table, eating a thick sandwich of bread and cold baked beans. The glass of milk at his elbow was half empty.

Captain Ben pulled his rocker into the sun and sat down heavily, lighting his pipe. "Have a good time last night?" he asked.

Jud swallowed rapidly. He didn't lift his head but leaned down to pat Skipper. "It was all right," he said slowly. Then he took a big drink of milk and put down the empty glass.

"Mr. York came in today," Captain Ben said. "Got a new outboard motor—a beauty too. Going to use it on the dinghy. He's looking for someone to take charge of it. Pretty good job for anyone who likes motors."

Jud didn't look at Captain Ben. He took his glass to the sink and washed it carefully, drying it on the clean linen towel, which he returned to its proper place on the rod behind the stove. Then he went to the door, followed by Skipper. "I'll be seeing you," he said in a toneless kind of voice, and went out, shutting the door quietly.

The men on the dock said, "Hi," to Jud when he came down to get his dory, but nothing more. He could feel them watching him, and he was sure that they all knew about Homer's boathouse windows. He kept his shoulders very straight and rowed away quickly, heading for Nubbin.

Once he had landed on the island he found it strangely uncomforting. It was his place, sure enough. He put his hand on a two-by-four and gave it a little shove. It was firm and true. The view across the tumbling waters was his. Turning to the east, he could hear the thump of hammers, which meant that shutters were being removed from the York house. A thin spiral of blue smoke rose from its chimneys. Mr. York was back, and he had a new outboard motor, and he wanted someone to run it.

"If I could run that motor," Jud said to Skipper. "If I could just run that motor for Mr. York!"

He sat down on a rock and stared out to sea, his heart full of wishes mixed up with hopelessness. After a long time he saw Homer's boat round the Point and turn into the harbor. In a few minutes he'd be at the dock, and everyone would talk about those darned windows. If only he, Jud, hadn't got mad and busted those windows! It was a dumb thing to do. He got up slowly and rowed back to the harbor. He noticed that Homer's boat was at the mooring, his dory pulled up on the shore. Gritting his teeth hard, the boy made himself go ashore and walk up to the boathouse.

Homer stood just inside the big door that faced the harbor. Jud looked at him and at the bright pieces of glass lying on the dirt floor. "Hi," he said gruffly. "It was an awful dumb thing to do, busting those windows." His voice was so unnatural that Skipper, standing close to him, whined a little, as if he were miserable too.

Homer looked at him for a long time. He lit a cigarette and blew a cloud into the still air. "Yeah," he said at last. "Kind of dumb. Maybe I was kind of dumb too, taking Dianne to Hardwick." He turned and looked at the windows. "We're both of us smart about some things," he said, almost smiling. "I'm just smart enough to have the money to buy the glass. Think you're smart enough to help me put it in?"

Jud nodded silently. He came a little nearer to Homer and held out his hand. They shook hands briefly, and the young man threw down his cigarette, stamping it out carefully. "Tomorrow?" he asked. "Tomorrow, when I get in from the traps?"

Jud nodded again and went back to his dory. Skipper

was slow to get into the boat and stood looking at the boy, his head on one side in a puzzled kind of way.

"It's all right, fella," Jud said, ruffling the little dog's coat with one hand. Skipper, comforted, jumped into the dory, barking happily.

Jud suddenly felt ten pounds lighter. It was all very well for Homer to say he had the money to buy the glass for those windows, but—

"If I could get that job with Mr. York," Jud said aloud, "if I could earn that money, I'd pay for it myself." Then he headed for Nubbin Island.

The little camp was fine now. Jud put up some shelves in one corner, fitting them neatly and spreading clean pieces of an old *Maine Coast Fisherman* on them. The work went well, and he looked about with pleasure.

"If I had a bunk, a small one," he said, "it would be super. And if I had a stove. . . . Oh, I really want that job with Mr. York!" He went outside and looked over to Easterly Point. Ladder Moore was there with a wheelbarrow, on which Captain Lu was piling firewood from the piles stacked in the woods. There were other men moving about. Every now and then Mr. York would come out of the house to talk and laugh with them, as if the job of getting settled was the pleasantest one in the world.

Suddenly Jud narrowed his eyes. He recognized two men who almost never were seen on Easterly Point. One was Captain Ben. He wasn't working but had found a stump near the house and had settled down there with his pipe as comfortably as if he were in his rocking chair at home.

Beside him, leaning against a tall spruce, and smoking, stood Homer, a broad grin on his face. Mr. York came out on the porch and stood talking earnestly to them. Jud's heart sank. Mr. York must be hearing about the boathouse windows. He'd never get that job now. Captain Ben wouldn't think much of it either. Gosh, what a stupid thing he had done!

Then, suddenly, he remembered the evening when he had looked up into Dianne's laughing face as he started to get into the cab. "It wasn't fair," he said. But he could hear clearly Homer's voice as it sounded that morning.

"I was kind of dumb too." Homer had said.

Jud squared his shoulders and pushed his dory into the channel, Skipper jumping in ahead of him. Either he could get that job with Mr. York or he couldn't. There was no point in sitting around thinking about it. He pulled hard at the oars, heading the dory for Easterly Point.

"I can *ask*," he said to Skipper. "There's no harm in *asking*."

6. Jud Gets a Job, and Does a Job

IT WAS quiet on Easterly Point when Jud, sitting on
the porch steps of the big house, looked into the
face of the tall man beside him, waiting for an
answer. Mr. York had a piece of soft pine which he
turned in his long fingers as he whittled it. Somewhere
in the village someone was chopping firewood into stove
lengths, and the thud of the ax echoed in the shadows.
Offshore, the steady put-put of a boat's motor meant
the return of a lobsterman from his traps. Inside the
house there was an occasional rustle of paper or clatter
of dishes as Mrs. York went briskly about the task of
getting settled.

Jud cleared his throat. "Please, Mr. York, could I
have that job? I can learn quick, honest I can."

Mr. York looked down at the face turned so hopefully
to him. He had heard about the broken windows from
Homer, who had also said he had been "dumb," as he
put it, about the trip to Hardwick. The man understood
why Jud had been so angry and hurt, but the violent
destruction of property bothered him. Besides, he had

heard the rumors about the boy being "light-fingered."
He turned the whittled piece of wood in his hand.

"Guess you heard I broke the windows down to
Homer's boathouse," the boy said in a low voice.

Mr. York looked at him quickly. "Suppose you tell
me about it," he said quietly.

"I broke them, that's all," Jud answered in a hopeless
tone of voice. "If you let me have the job, I couldn't
start on it for a week, anyway. I'm going to help Homer
put the lights in."

Mr. York nodded. Good kid, he thought. He isn't
going to blame anyone else for what happened. He did
wrong and he's going to take the blame for it and do
the best he can to set things right.

He stood up quickly. "I'll be too busy here on the
place to do much boating this week anyway," he said,
as if he had suddenly made up his mind. "I guess you've
got a job, if you want it," he went on, and held out his
hand.

Jud stood up and slipped his small brown hand into
the big strong grasp offered him. Mr. York held the boy's
hand fast and looked soberly into his eyes. "No getting
mad on this job," he said firmly. "If you don't understand anything I ask you to do, just tell me. I'm not a
hard man to get along with, but I came down here for
a pleasant time. I don't want to have to nag at you or
check up on you all the time. I'll teach you how to run
the motor and take care of it. I'll tell you what your

duties are and what your pay will be. Then it's up to you."

Jud's eyes grew large. "Do you mean," he asked in a half-frightened voice, "that I'm *responsible*?"

Mr. York laughed a little and dropped his hand. "That's it," he said lightly. "We'll get along fine—you'll see." Then he turned and went into the house.

In the week that followed, Jud was up every morning at six. Although Homer had gone to his traps by the time the boy reached the boathouse, there was work to be done before the glass could be set. All the broken glass had to be picked up carefully, of course. Then the dry, crumbly putty had to be scraped out thoroughly and the wood frames sandpapered.

"Might as well do this right," Homer had said, eying the muntins and frames, which had never been painted and which were worn by wind and weather.

"Might as well do this right," Homer repeated. "We'll put a thin coat of creosote on all the exposed surfaces to preserve them." He opened the big can of stain and showed Jud how to stir it and thin it.

Each day the boy stuck faithfully to the job of preparation, until Homer came in from his traps. Then they would set a few lights before it was time for supper. As each window had twelve lights, and three windows had been either cracked or broken, it was long, tedious work. Jud's back and arms ached from all the sanding and scraping. His hair bleached almost white under the warming sun of June, and his skin was tanned. Then, on a Thursday, it was *done!*

The new lights had been washed and polished after they were set, and they glittered brightly in the reflection from the harbor. Jud carried the putty and knife and scraper into the boathouse and put them on a shelf, stomping the top of the putty can down hard with the heel of his hand. He covered the creosote can the same way and put it away. Then he turned to Homer with a tired smile.

"Looks good, doesn't it?" he asked. The young man nodded. "Tell you one thing," the boy went on. "I'll *never* bust another window in my whole life! I'm going to pay for the lights," he said. "The very first pay I'll get I'll pay for those lights."

Homer reached down into a keg filled with cold salt water and pulled out two bottles of pop. He tossed one to Jud. "Catch," he said.

Sitting on the hump of grass and sand beside the boathouse door, Jud felt the knots in his back and arms come untied. Homer took a long thirsty drink of pop, looking at the boy over the tilted bottle.

"You can pay half," he agreed. "You'll get good money, working for Mr. York, and he's a good man to work for. He'll want things done his way, and sometimes it won't be your way at all. But if it comes out wrong he'll be the first one to say he made a mistake." He

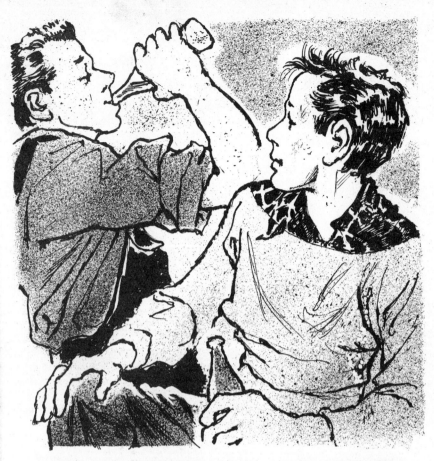

paused, drank some more pop, and asked, "What are you going to do with all that money?"

Jud hesitated. Homer must be all right. He had helped build the camp. He had felt bad about the way the celebration had turned out. Maybe he could be trusted to understand.

"First," the boy said slowly, "I wanted to pay back the town for the money they've spent on me. But Captain Ben says I can do that if I want to when I'm a grown man." He paused for a minute. Then he went on firmly. "I want to get a stove, a kind of small stove, and a length of pipe for my camp. I want it more than any-thing else in the world."

Homer nodded as if he understood perfectly. "You'll get your stove," he said soberly, "if you want it hard enough. You'll get your stove, all right."

7. Someone New in Town

THE following three weeks were the busiest and best Jud had ever known. He had been scared at first when Mr. York took down the shining blue and aluminum motor from the rack he had installed in a small storage room on the dock. The boy had, of course, seen outboards before, but never one as new and expensive-looking. There had been a great deal to learn, but Mr. York was patient and never hurried.

"Be sure you understand what I tell you and why it must be done as I say," Mr. York had said the first day, and Jud asked so many questions that he began to feel as if there were nothing in the world but a big blue and silver motor. He thought about it at breakfast, dinner, and supper, and even dreamed about it.

It was just as Homer had said: Jud had to carry out Mr. York's orders exactly, even as to how to carry the motor and how to set it down on the dock. He learned how to mix the proper proportions of gasoline and oil, and how to keep the fuel tank and gasoline clean. After a few days he found himself automatically checking the angle of the drive shaft to the surface of the water when he put the motor in place on the stern of the dinghy. Then he had to master the gear shift and learn how to reverse. Mr. York gave him a small metal box with a tight-fitting cover in which to keep extra supplies like spark plugs, shear pins, and cord for the starter.

"Never forget your extra supplies," Mr. York said almost sternly. "The time you leave them ashore will be the time you'll need them most."

At last, after hours of drilling and practicing, Mr. York stepped from the dinghy to the dock. "Take her out alone, Jud," he said. "Take her around the harbor and then bring her in through the moorings to the dock."

Jud's heart beat hard against his ribs. He glanced up at the old captains on the bench, who were watching him closely. The younger men at the pound had stopped their work and stood watching too. The boy's face tightened. He'd show them all.

He looked at Mr. York. "If I'm doing all right, may I let her out a little on the way into the harbor, and may I take Skipper?" he asked.

The man smiled and nodded. "Don't come in fast through the moorings, son," he said. "But you can let her out a little farther out. And you may take Skipper."

Jud will never forget that first time alone with the outboard. His fears disappeared entirely. He felt as if he had been doing this all his life. When he "let her out,"

the dinghy shot ahead fast enough to send a fine spray
of water into his face, and the wake behind the propeller
boiled up in a splendid way. When he came in to the
moorings he slowed down to a very gentle speed and
slid into the landing at the dock as easily as he would
have done in his dory.

"*Not* bad," said Mr. York. "Not bad at all."

After that first, glorious trip, the job settled down to a comfortable routine. Each morning Jud reported at the Easterly Point house to see if there were any errands to be done at Hardwick, or if a sailing expedition was to be planned. If not, he went to the dock and swabbed out the dinghy and rowed it out to the big sloop. He never took Skipper to the sloop, for there was no way of getting around the fact that a small dog could track an awful lot of dirt.

Part of Jud's job was to keep the sloop in shining and immaculate order, ropes neatly coiled, sails dried out after rain or fog, decks dry, and cabin well aired. If the outboard motor had been used he had to drain out the "old" gasoline and refill the tank, wipe the motor carefully, check the amount of lubricant in the gear-case, or perhaps clean the sparkplugs. When he felt that his job was done for the day he could quit.

"I'm not keeping a time clock on you," Mr. York had said.

So there was time for the camp on Nubbin, time for the chores at home, time—and money too—for a trip or two with Homer to Hardwick for the movies. Jud felt *good*. Mr. York wasn't given to praising people, but you could tell that he thought the boy was doing a good job. The old men on the wharf spoke to the boy differently now, as though they thought he was pretty smart. Yes, Jud felt good. He had paid for the broken lights first thing. And every week he gave Captain Ben all his pay but one dollar which he kept for pocket money. The old man put the money away carefully in his lock box.

The boy was so busy these days that it was with considerable surprise that he realized, shortly after he got his job, that there was a newcomer in the village. One afternoon after work he rowed down to the boathouses to see if Homer had come in from his traps. He heard a splashing sound ahead of him. Skipper, in the bow of the dory, barked excitedly. Jud turned his head to look over his shoulder in the direction of the splashing. Maybe a seal had come in close on the high tide or a gull had made a deep dive for a fish.

At first the boy saw nothing. Then he saw a long, tanned arm lift out of the water and make a powerful stroke. Someone was swimming strongly and steadily. Now no one, Jud would have said, no one with any sense goes swimming off Spruce Point's shores. Even in July the water is as cold as a knife, and merely wading around to haul in a boat numbs your feet and legs so that they hurt.

Jud pulled hard on his oars and came alongside the swimmer. He was a young man with dark hair and eyes, a stranger whom the boy had never seen before. As the swimmer turned his head above the water he sighted the boat and stopped swimming, seeming to stand upright in the water.

"Hi," Jud said, and, out of sheer amazement, asked, "Are you touching bottom way out here?"

The young man laughed and shook his head. "No," he said, "I'm treading water."

Jud was about to ask what that meant but thought better of it. It must be what Skipper did to keep afloat. "Isn't the water cold?" he asked.

"It's *good*," the young man said. He turned on one side and lifted his hand. "I'll be seeing you!" he called and swam off.

Easy as a fish, Jud said to himself. Must be sort of fun to swim like that, real steady, without getting tired. Then he rowed into shore.

Homer was at the boathouse, turning over a damaged trap. He looked up as the boy came toward him. "D'you see that feller?" Jud asked excitedly. "D'you see the way he swims? Where'd he come from? I've never seen him before. Is he from Hardwick?"

Homer shook his head. "Nope," he said. "He's an old Spruce Pointer, he is. Born here, anyways. His pa and ma came here from down Jonesport way a long time ago. Lived up the road beyond Bryants'. They stayed here until he finished school. Had an awful smart pa. A real good fisherman, name of Ed Fontaine. This one's name is Tom." Homer paused and turned the trap over. "Tom never cared about fishing and lobstering," he said slowly, shaking his head as if there were something wrong with such a man.

Jud understood. He'd heard the men in the village talking many times, shaking their heads over men in Hardwick who had no use for traps and boats or the long hard fight to earn a living on the water. Queer, he thought to himself.

"Well," he said, "Mr. York isn't a fisherman, and all he wants of a boat is to cruise her, not to work her, but *he's* all right."

"Oh, sure," Homer said quickly. "But he wasn't born here. His folks didn't come from here. But Tom Fontaine's did. They say he worked on his folks to move to Boston so he could go to high school and college. All he was interested in was books," he concluded almost scornfully.

"I sort of like books—some books," Jud said in a low voice. "I can see how Tom Fontaine could like books a lot."

Homer clapped the boy on the shoulder. "You win," he said cheerfully. "But no matter how many books you read, you'll never want to get away from the water, I know that." He paused. "Say," he said slowly, "you can't call Tom Fontaine 'Tom' or even 'Mister Fontaine,' in case you have occasion to call him anything."

"I can't?" Jud asked in bewilderment. "What can I call him?"

"You call him 'Father Fontaine,'" Homer replied. "If

you get to know him real well, you can call him 'Father Tom.' His folks were Catholics, and he's a priest. Teaches in a college up in Boston."

Jud's mouth fell wide open. He didn't know much about Catholics except that in some unexplained way they were "different." He knew even less about priests, except that they were 'specially "different." They couldn't be just *people*, he thought—people who could swim as easy as a fish and talked like anybody—no airs or anything.

"I'll be darned," he said slowly. "I'll be gosh-darned." He felt sort of scared. Why, he'd been talking to this— this "Father Tom" as if he were just anybody.

He turned on his heel and started back to his boat. Before he shoved off, he paused to shout to Homer. "Well," he called, "he's an awful good swimmer!"

8. The Wonderful Week

THE next week "it came off hawt," as Captain Ben would say. A strong offshore wind blew steadily, bringing with it waves of dry, sun-baked air. It didn't take many hours of this to make Mr. York decide on a 'long-shore cruise. When Jud appeared at the Yorks' on Tuesday morning he was given a long list of errands and chores connected with getting the sloop ready.

"You help us get off, Jud," Mr. York said, "and keep an eye on the place while we're gone, and you'll get your regular pay. We won't be gone more than a week —ten days at the most."

So all day and into the evening Jud scurried about, until, as the round orange moon rose out of the sea, all was ready for taking off at an early hour the next morning.

After the sloop had left the harbor the next day Jud suddenly felt lost. He had become so used to having a job that he didn't know quite what to do with himself. He rowed out to Nubbin Island and opened his camp and figured where he'd put his little stove when he got it. He sawed up one of the trees he had cut down and made a low bench to use in front of the stove.

When the job was done he felt hot and sweaty. Without any real purpose in mind, he rowed down the shore toward Homer's boathouse. As he drew near, he heard again a familiar steady splashing and, looking over his shoulder, saw Father Tom swimming toward him. As the young man drew near, Jud looked at him enviously.

"That looks awful cool!" he said.

"It is. It's wonderful," Father Tom said, catching hold of the gunwale. "Why don't you come in too?"

Jud hesitated. For the first time in his life he was not satisfied to be unable to swim. "I'm not much of a swimmer," he said slowly.

"You don't have to be much of a swimmer in this water," Father Tom said. "It's so full of salt that it holds you up like a life preserver. There's a pair of trunks up in Homer's boathouse. He'd let you borrow them. Come on in!"

The trunks were a little big for the boy, but he strung a piece of rope through the belt loops and pulled it tight around his skinny waist. When he went across the pebbly beach to the water the hot sun felt good on his back and shoulders. Skipper was very troubled at first, when Jud waded into the tingly water. The dog dashed up and down the beach, barking, and finally waded in until he was beyond his depth and found himself swimming. Jud followed the excited little dog, feeling a little frightened.

He didn't do much more for a while but splash and

dog-paddle, watching the strong, even strokes made by the tall young man and wishing he could really swim.

Finally he asked, "How do you make your feet go? You don't splash with them at all." To his surprise, Father Tom left the deep water and headed in to where the shore dropped off gradually. Jud and Skipper followed him.

"Flop down here beside me," Father Tom said, stretching out on his stomach in the shallow water. "Now watch, and do just as I do."

For more than an hour Jud practiced the stretching and pulling motion of his arms, the slow twisting of his body and turning of his head, and the regular treading of his feet—which Father Tom called a "crawl." Then the two of them went out to where the water was up to Jud's waist, and he tried his new skills there. He got water up his nose; he swallowed water; he kept touching bottom with his feet. But finally, late in the afternoon, for three whole strokes, Jud *swam!*

Father Tom was as pleased as Jud was. He was almost as tired. He shook himself like a big dog and picked up his towel and robe from the beach. The boy pulled on his blue jeans and hung up the trunks to dry. Then he wearily rowed the young priest to the dock. He felt wonderful.

As they came up to the dock, one of the men who was shutting up the lobster pound shouted, "Hey, there, Jud, was that you swimming down the shore?"

Jud nodded.

"He'll be a good swimmer if he keeps on," Father Tom said, and Jud felt as if he were suddenly six feet tall.

That was the beginning of a wonderful week. Every day, and sometimes twice a day, Jud had a swimming lesson. Each day he felt more sure of himself and learned more than just how to keep afloat. In between swimming lessons Jud sat on the beach, or listened.

The young priest was a science teacher in Boston, and he told the boy a great many things about the planets and stars, about what people could learn from such ordinary things as the shells along the shore and the great flat rocks to the east of the village. Sometimes there was no talk at all; Jud would lie face down on the pebbly sand, half asleep, listening to the sea, while Father Tom read quietly to himself out of a small black book.

It was a queer, good-feeling thing, Jud thought sleepily to himself. He'd never had a friend like this before. Homer had helped him build the camp, but the boy suspected that he could and would be dropped like a hotcake if Homer had anything better to do. But Father Tom seemed to have all the time in the world for Jud.

He likes me and Skipper, the boy thought. He doesn't know what they think about me in this town.

As a matter of fact, the young priest had heard all that "they" said. He boarded with the Bryants and had, of course, been told by them about the broken windows at the boathouse. He had also been told the familiar story that Jud was "light-fingered" and couldn't be trusted. He had had to listen, but he had made no comment. When they told him how it happened that Jud was boarded by the town with Captain Ben, he had said quietly, "A boy needs a family," as if he were remembering the loss of his own father and mother.

9. Jud Sees His Stove

IF THE weather had held until the Yorks came back, things might have been different. On Saturday, however, there was a sudden change of wind. It "came off East" early in the day, bringing with it great clouds of thick fog and a chilling dampness.

Father Tom sat by the fire at Bryants', reading and writing letters. Jud didn't expect anyone to go swimming on such a day, so he put on his boots and oilskins and rowed out to Nubbin. Skipper shivered and kept close to Jud. This was a day when the island, with the rocks slippery with dampness and the branches of the trees wet with fog, was no fun for a little dog. It was shadowy and damp there too, and Jud thought yearningly of the little stove that would have made it so snug and comfortable a place. He came out of the camp and looked over to the Yorks'. He ought to go over to see if everything was all right. Mr. York had told him to do so. He pushed the dory away from the island and rowed over to Easterly Point.

As soon as the nose of the dory touched shore Skipper shot off into the woods, leaping and barking with excitement over the delightful smells he found there.

Everything was tight at the big house—windows latched, doors locked, and hatchways fastened. The garage was padlocked, as usual. Someone had gathered a pile of brushwood and left it in the garage driveway. Although the Yorks almost never used their car, the brushwood would have to be moved before the garage doors could be opened. Jud began methodically to pick up armfuls of the tight, dry wood and to make a new pile behind the garage. It was a long, tedious job. Once, when Jud stopped to stretch his aching arms, he had a queer feeling that someone was around and near by, that someone was watching him.

"Hi there!" he called out, but no one answered. After a minute or two he started in again, and very soon he had cleared the driveway.

Then he went to the two long sheds used for storage. The first was used for boat gear, Jud knew. It was firmly padlocked, and the shutters were closed and locked on the inside. The second shed was used for what Mr. York called his "antiques." The door was locked; the east and south windows were latched. There was one window in the west wall. To Jud's surprise, the glass was broken. It had not smashed or cracked, but there was a hole about the size of a quarter just above the inside lock. You could put your finger in, easy as pie, and turn that latch and push the window up. Without thinking at all, Jud turned the latch, opened the window, and climbed over the sill.

The shed was pretty well filled, but there was room enough to move around. The boy felt his way about carefully until his eyes grew used to the dark shadows and shapes around him. Groping past the door, he touched a key hanging on a long cord beside the door frame. Along one wall there were several straight chairs and a pile of cartons packed with small objects wrapped in newspapers. Some old kerosene lamps stood on a battered table. Beside them was a pile of patchwork quilts covered with a piece of sailcloth. There were two or three old chests of drawers pushed together, and next to them—Jud drew in his breath sharply—*four* old-fashioned stoves!

In a minute he was down on his knees by them, pushing them about a little to measure them by the feel of his hands. The last stove in the row he knew at once to be *his* stove, the one that was just right for his camp. Exploring in his pants pockets, Jud found three wooden matches. He jiggled each of the lamps on the table gently until he heard the faint slosh of kerosene in the base of one of them. Then, with infinite care, he managed to get a faint, flickering light going. He carried the lamp very steadily to the end of the shed where the stoves were and set it down on the floor. Then he knelt down to look at his stove.

It was a real, sure-enough stove, for all its smallness. It stood about sixteen inches off the floor on four sturdy claw-shaped feet. There was no oven, but in its place was a door through which the firewood was pushed to rest on a grate above a heavy iron floor. The top of the stove, Jud figured, was about a foot square, with four little stove lids no bigger than saucers. Behind the stove, leaning against the shed wall, was a small stovepipe about five feet long.

Jud touched the cold iron with gentle, loving hands. There wasn't a crack in it. On the little shelf at one side there was even a small lifter for the stove lids.

"You're perfect," Jud breathed. "You're just *perfect!*"

Then, once again, he felt as if someone were watching him. He went to the window, which he had left open an inch. But there was nothing to be seen except the dark branches of pine trees and the swirling fog. He went back to the stove, turning it about, lifting the lids and setting them back neatly. The gentle clink of iron on iron sounded loud in the stillness.

"I wish you were mine," Jud said in a whisper. "You little beauty, I wish you were mine."

Suddenly he could see how easy it would be. He could lift the stove easily, carry it to the door, which could be unlocked from the inside, and set the stove out on the ground. Then he could lock the door, return the key to its cord, and climb out of the window. In no time at all he could carry the stove down to his dory and row it over to Nubbin. Before supper that very day he could set it up and have a small bright fire in his camp. For a long moment the picture he had conjured up was so tempting that he pulled the little stove toward him. Then he dropped his arms. He rubbed his eyes and shook his head.

"So far," he said aloud, "so far nothing they've said about me—nothing bad—has been true. But suppose it *was* true—suppose Father Tom and Mr. York and

Captain Ben all knew it was true!" He turned, not daring to look at the little stove again.

"I've got to get out of here," Jud whispered. He carried the lamp quickly to the table where he had found it, lowered the wick, and blew out the flickering flame. In the sudden darkness of the shed the fading light coming in the west windows stood out sharply. In a second he had pushed the window open and scrambled out, running as fast as he could to his dory.

As he pushed off he heard a faint sound. It was as if someone were laughing in the darkening woods, a foolish kind of laugh. Jud listened hard, but the sound was not repeated. Had there been someone there all the time, listening and watching?

The woods were still. The sea made a small whispering sound on the shore. Jud called for Skipper once or twice, but the little dog was too far away to hear him. Oh well, he would find his way home. The boy pushed off from the shore and rowed slowly to the dock.

10. Fire!

As Jud rowed to the dock he felt as if part of him were still in the shed close to the stove. Perhaps it wasn't Mr. York's favorite and someday he would sell it. The boy remembered how it had looked in the flickering light of the small lamp.

Suddenly he pulled hard on the oars. He hadn't closed and fastened that window in the west wall of the shed. He should have figured out some way to wedge it tight. He should have stuffed something—an old rag or leaves—into that hole so there'd be no chance of rain blowing in. He rowed as fast as he could to the dock, tide up the dory, and ran down the path to Easterly Point.

As Jud came out of the clearing in back of Mr. York's place he could see that there was a light in the shed. But he had put out the lamp—he *knew* he had. He remembered turning down the wick and blowing out the flame. He ran to the west wall of the shed, and, to his horror, saw a steady funnel of smoke coming from the broken window. With his bare hands he smashed the glass completely and plunged over the sill. The rubble of paper and excelsior on the floor was blazing brightly and traveling fast to the cartons stored at one end.

Jud jumped across the flame, pulled away the canvas over the quilts, and slapped it down on the fire. The smoke was very thick now, and he saw the flames running out from one end of the canvas. This was no time to spare the quilts, he knew. He spread first one and then another on the ground, stamping out the flames under them. His hands were bleeding now from the cuts he had hardly noticed when he broke the window. The flames had scorched one leg of his jeans, and the flesh under it hurt dreadfully. The thick smoke choked him, making him cough and feel sick and dizzy.

But the fire was out—really out. The quilts were hot under the soles of his sneakers, but there was no fire. All of a sudden, even as he heard voices shouting, pain and dizziness swept over him like a wave and down he fell on the quilts, as if to the bottom of the sea.

The night that followed was never very clear in Jud's memory. Somebody carried him to Captain Ben's and laid him gently on the old sofa in the kitchen. The doctor came from Hardwick and stuck a needle into his arm to make the pain go away. He must have slept while his singed clothes were carefully cut off. His hands were bandaged and his burns were dressed, but the boy knew nothing about it.

When he awoke, it was nearly noon. Captain Ben was sitting in the old rocking chair, reading the paper and glancing over the top of it at Jud every now and then. Seeing that the boy was awake, he got out of his chair slowly and went over to the sofa.

"Feeling better?" he asked gruffly. "Want something to eat?"

Jud shook his head a little. "I'm thirsty," he whispered.

Captain Ben got some water and fed it to him very slowly with a spoon. Skipper, who had been lying close by, stood and put his front paws up on the foot of the sofa.

"Do you hurt bad?" the old man asked anxiously.

Jud didn't answer. He hurt all over, as a matter of fact. He just wanted to sleep. He shut his eyes. Something was wrong about the kitchen, he thought vaguely. Where was Miz Hanks? Well, it didn't matter. Once more he fell asleep.

By five o'clock the boy was awake and ready for food. Miz Hanks had not appeared, but there was a fine smell of fish chowder in the room. Captain Ben fed him almost a bowlful, and then sat down with his own bowl of chowder and some crusty bread.

Jud followed him with his eyes. Though he still didn't feel like talking, there was something he had to say. "Captain Ben," he said slowly, "I wasn't doing anything wrong. I was just seeing if everything was okay for Mr. York." He stopped, feeling awfully tired.

The old man looked at him steadily. "Guess you were sort of scared, weren't you?" he asked.

Jud sighed deeply. "I can't tell anyone, ever, how scared I was," he answered. "I looked in the window and there was the fire racing across the floor." Jud began to shiver from head to foot.

"There, there," Captain Ben said hastily, "I've been scared. Everybody's been scared at one time or another. The trick is to *do* something in spite of being scared. And you did."

Jud forgot he was twelve years old, and began to cry softly.

Captain Ben shoved his rocker over beside the sofa. He sat down in it, tilted back, and put his feet up on the shelf of the stove. He lit his pipe and then put one hand very gently on the coverlet spread over the boy.

"I was a grown man," he said slowly, "a grown man with seven years aboard ship behind me, when I was so scared I didn't think I'd live to tell it. We were all scared, shivering, sick scared. 'Most sixty years ago, it was, but I feel a cold chill now, remembering it." For a moment the old man seemed to draw nearer to the warmth of the stove. Then he went on.

"I was aboard the *Yosemite* out of Gloucester, one of the finest vessels ever built. We set out for Newfoundland in the dead of winter, with Captain McKinnon as master. We made it up there all right, but on the way home we ran into a heavy gale of wind from the southeast and a blinding snowstorm. We were all on deck as the vessel scudded along—going twelve knots an hour, I'll wager. First thing any of us knew she brought up with a dreadful grinding crash on a ledge, with most of the bottom knocked out of her.

" 'Take to the rigging!' someone yelled, and we were aloft, every man of us, quicker'n I can tell it. In an hour's time the waves had done their worst, and the *Yosemite* broke squarely in two. Down cracked the mainmast, taking most of the foremast with it. One of the men struck out in that wicked sea for a rock, and we all scrambled after. Though the water was breaking over the rock, we had no real hopes of reaching it. But we made it and managed to climb up on it. Pieces of wood from the vessel swept out to us, and we snatched at them, driving them into cracks in the rock for hand holds and footholds so we wouldn't get swept off."

Captain Ben knocked out his pipe and began to fill it very carefully. He glanced at Jud, who was lying very still, his eyes fixed on the old man.

"There were nine of us on that rock, not much longer than this kitchen," Captain Ben said slowly. "The sea tore at us and the snow blinded us and it was dark— dark as flugion."

Jud blinked. "Flugion" was a new word to him, but this was no time to bother about words. He knew it must have been awfully dark on that rock.

"Captain McKinnon's leg was hurt bad and another fellow had both his legs broken, but we hung on, waiting for daylight," Captain Ben continued. "After what seemed like a hundred years, the day came and we could see that we had stove up off Ram's Island. Between the rock we were on and the island was another ledge, bare now, because the tide was low. All through the morning and early afternoon we hung on and hoped for rescue. With the prospect of night coming on, and high water with it, Captain McKinnon called to his mate, Pat Rose.

" 'Another night will mean death, Pat,' he said.

"Pat nodded solemnly but said not a word. I knew he was a strong swimmer, but I feared for him when he stood up on the rock and pulled off his heavy clothes. The sea was still running strong, and we were all weak from strain.

" 'It's no use, boys,' he said, 'it's no use to stay here to die. I'll take the chances for you.' And he struck out for the other ledge. It was a hard battle, but he made it. When we saw him go from the ledge through shallow water to the island, we did our best to cheer, but our voices were lost in the wind.

"Pat ran along the beach to a boathouse. Surely he'd find help there. He wasn't gone long, but waded back slowly to the inner ledge and shouted to us. 'You'll have to swim for it,' he yelled, 'there's no help here!'

"All day we had tried to grab the *Yosemite*'s log line, without success. Now, by a miracle, I caught it and grasped it firmly. I passed it around my waist and made it fast. Then out I plunged into the sea, floundering, splashing, and kicking my way to Pat's outstretched hands. He hauled me up. We fastened a stouter rope from the vessel to the log line and on this the men came in, hand over hand.

"Cold and well-nigh starving, we made it to the boathouse. I took off my coat and hung it on a pole raised on the shore for a signal. The island was only a mile and a half from the Nova Scotia mainland. Surely when the snow abated, someone would come for us."

Captain Ben turned in his chair and looked at Jud. The boy's eyes were closing, but when the story seemed to have ended they opened wide. "What then?" he asked sleepily.

"They saw our signal, all right," Captain Ben said, "but the sea was too rough to launch a boat. Think of it, boy, too rough for a boat, but Pat Rose had gone into that welter to save us all." He shook his head as if he could hardly believe his own memory. "Pat was scared, for only a fool would not have feared that sea," the old man said almost in a whisper. "But he wasn't so scared he couldn't *do* something about it." He glanced at Jud. The boy was asleep once more, and the room was very still. Skipper lay close beside him, his nose just touching a bandaged hand.

For a little while Captain Ben sat staring into the bright coals, remembering. Then he heard footsteps coming around the house. He got up and went to the door, opening it carefully. Father Tom stood on the step. The old man motioned to him to come in, pointing to the sleeping boy.

"They want you at the schoolhouse," Father Tom said in a whisper. "I'll sit with Jud while you're gone. You go along."

Captain Ben looked at Jud. Then he looked at Father Tom. "He didn't do anything wrong," he whispered. "I know he didn't do anything wrong."

11. Father Tom and Captain Ben Stand By

URING the quiet hour while Jud slept, Father Tom sat in the big rocker near by and thought about the meeting that was taking place at the school and about the boy who had become his friend. He read from the small prayer book he always carried, and was sitting with his eyes closed when Jud woke up.

"Father Tom!" Jud cried in a small, surprised voice. He stretched out his bandaged hand, and Father Tom laid his long, tanned fingers lightly on top of it.

"Captain Ben had to go out for a little while," the young man said. "So I came to keep you and Skipper company. I was glad to see you sleeping so quietly, because it meant you weren't suffering. You've had a hard time." He paused. "Nobody in the village seems to know exactly what happened," he went on. "Want to talk about it?"

Jud moved restlessly. "There was a fire in the shed,"

he said slowly. Then he was silent, as if he were trying to figure something out. "Father Tom," he asked, "how could there have been a fire in that shed? What do they say in the village? Has anyone said how it started? Does anyone know?" The questions came thick and fast, as if he'd been thinking of them during the time he had been sleeping.

Father Tom shook his head. He looked troubled, and he hesitated a long moment before he answered. "There's a lot of talk," he said. "Everybody's talking. But all they know is that you were there. They think you were awfully lucky to put it out so quickly." His voice sounded unhappy. "You know how scared people here are of fire," he added quickly. "You can't blame them, when the nearest fire-fighting equipment is in Hardwick."

Jud pulled himself painfully up in bed. He seized Father Tom's wrist with both his bandaged hands. His face was suddenly flushed, and his eyes were very bright. "What are they *saying*?" he demanded in a rough voice. "Are they saying I started the fire—that it was my fault?"

Father Tom met his eyes squarely. "Some of them say that, Jud," he answered quietly.

Jud threw himself back on the pillows. He put one arm over his eyes. His shoulders shook a little. "There's not any use," he said. "I've tried and tried but they don't care. The first thing that happens, they blame it on me." He sobbed once and then bit his lip hard. In a minute he put his arm around Skipper and stared at the young man, his eyes very bright. "What was the point of trying so hard?" he cried.

Father Tom hesitated once more. "People have been asking that question for a long, long time, Jud," he said slowly. "Not just boys like you, but grown men and women who try hard." The room was very quiet. "Do you remember your father, Jud?" The young man asked gently.

Jud shook his head. "Not really," he said. "Just things like once he carried me home on his back when there was deep snow. Things like that. He was brave, though. Everyone said he was awful brave, hanging onto the man who got swept overboard until a big wave carried them both off."

Father Tom looked at the flickering coals. "He tried to do what was right, and he died trying," he said, almost as if he were talking to himself.

"That's what I mean," Jud said almost angrily. "There's no point in trying."

"Well," said Father Tom, strongly and quietly, as if he believed with all his heart what he was saying, "it seems that way because we haven't talked at all about God's part in all this. If your father had been here while you were growing up, he would have wanted you to live by certain rules—such as when you could take out a boat, and how you must take care of it. Perhaps you wouldn't have seen any reason for some of the things he would have told you. God is the Father of every one of us, and He has rules too. He doesn't expect that they will always make sense to us. But He does expect us to try hard to live by His rules without complaining or questioning, because He knows much more about what is good for us than we do."

The young priest was silent, taking a little time to straighten the blankets at the foot of the old sofa. Then he said lightly, "You felt pretty good when you were trying, didn't you, Jud?"

Jud nodded. He lay quite still, thinking hard. As his eyes were closed, Father Tom thought he was asleep. After a little while, Jud spoke almost in a whisper. "I bet my father was just like you," he said softly.

Father Tom made no answer. When he looked at Jud again, the boy was really asleep and, to the young priest's great joy, he was smiling a little. Skipper stirred a little, licked the bandaged hand near him, and slept too.

When Captain Ben walked into the brightly lighted schoolroom, he was surprised to see so many disturbed and excited faces. They weren't all angry faces, he noticed. Miz Hanks was bustling about, her face quite set and red-looking. It was she who had called the village people together, Captain Ben knew. He sighed heavily. She had never liked Jud, resenting the extra washing and cleaning up after a boy, even a pretty good boy.

Captain Lu sat at the teacher's desk, his white duck captain's hat firmly set on his head as a mark of his position as town moderator. Also, in spite of a large sign lettered in red that said NO SMOKING, his pipe puffed clouds of smoke over his head.

Mrs. Gilley, still in the apron she wore in the store, was too round to squeeze into one of the seats fastened to a desk and had perched on the edge of a chair. Her cheeks were very pink, and she looked as if she had been crying.

Homer was sitting toward the front of the room. Captain Ben couldn't see his face, but his back was very straight and stubborn-looking.

Near him sat Mr. York, looking very tanned by sun and wind. He must have come back from his cruise that very day. When he turned his head to speak to Homer, Captain Ben tried to figure out how he had taken the fire, but his expression told very little about his feelings.

Way across the room were the Bryants. Sitting between her father and mother was Dianne, her hair tightly curled and wearing a good deal of lipstick. She looked mad and she kept her eyes fixed on the back of Homer's head. Captain Ben recalled some story Miz Hanks had repeated about her—that Homer had stopped taking her places.

The old man looked all around the room. Someone from almost every family in the village was there—the Bensons, the Lawlers, the Youngs, and the Fernalds. More women than men, the captain thought. Women sure liked to get out of the house! Against the far wall a tall, thin man leaned, his hands in his pockets. It was Ladder. He had been a hero all day, for he had called the village men to put out the fire. It had been an exciting feeling. Every now and then a man would clap him on the shoulder or a woman would speak admiringly to him, and he looked more and more pleased.

Poor Ladder, thought Captain Ben. There's not a mite

of harm in him. He'll never forget this time when the village was so proud of him. But— He frowned, troubled. But it was Jud who put the fire out. And he didn't— he couldn't—he *never* had any part in starting it.

Just then Captain Lu banged on the teacher's desk with a gavel. "This ain't a real town meeting," he began, "not called for the transaction of official business. But it seems a lot of folks got quite a scare out of the fire down to Yorks'. They want to sift out the why and wherefore of it. As Miz Hanks was the one who got the people all together here, I guess she should have the floor first."

Captain Ben's heart sank to his polished boots.

Miz Hanks stood up, her hands twisting in front of her the way they always did when she was mad or excited. "We're here to talk about the fire, and I guess there isn't much question about how it started," she snapped in a high, raspy voice.

Sounds like two marbles rubbed together, Captain Ben thought.

"When the men got down to Yorks', who did they find in the shed?" she asked. "You know as well as I do, they found that Jud," she went on. "If he didn't start it, what was he doing there?"

There was a murmur in the room.

"I'm not saying he did it a-purpose," she went on quickly. "It coulda been an accident. But he's a careless, heedless boy, with no thought for property. He's

been that way right along. I say—and there's lots of folks right in this room who agree with me—that that boy belongs in some kind of school where he'll have to learn to take care of things and leave other people's things alone. He just ain't to be trusted."

There was more low-voiced talking, and Miz Hanks looked to the back of the room toward Captain Ben. "I'm not saying," she went on, "that Captain Ben hasn't tried hard. If anything, he's been too good to a boy who's only a town charge. And, heaven only knows, I've done my best. I've tried to do my duty by him as a Christian. But the truth of the matter is, Jud's too much for either of us. He needs a strong, firm hand." Then she sat down, her thin shoulders twitching angrily.

Captain Ben cleared his throat. "Mr. Moderator," he began, "this seems to be out of order. We haven't heard the boy's story, and he can't get out of his bed to tell it. Why, 'tisn't American to judge a person less'n he can defend himself. As far as I can make out, Jud was down to Mr. York's place checking up on it." The old man raised his voice. "Mr. York," he asked, "did you ask Jud to keep an eye on your property while you were offshore?"

Mr. York stood up. "Mr. Moderator," he said, "checking up on my place was part of Jud's job. I think everyone here would say, as I do, that Jud's been a real responsible boy this summer." He paused, looking a little troubled. "I didn't give him any keys," he went on. "I don't know why he went into the shed. But I agree with Captain Ben that we shouldn't even discuss the fire until Jud can tell his story." Then he sat down.

The murmur ran around the room again. The people of Spruce Point were fair-minded enough, but they had been thoroughly frightened by the fire. The Bensons, whose place backed up to the Yorks, talked in low tones to their neighbors. Captain Ben sighed. They'd been scared, and now they were mad. They wanted to blame someone.

There was a stir in the front of the room. Mrs. Gilley was pulling herself to her feet. "I just want to say," she began, almost as if she were ready to cry again, "I don't believe that Jud started that fire, no matter what any- one says. He's lots more careful about fire than my boys were at his age. He helps me burn up grocery cartons and trash whenever it's fit weather for it. Lots of times he won't let me burn stuff when I want to. ' 'Tain't safe, Mrs. Gilley,' he'll say."

Then Homer got up slowly. He looked around the room for a long minute. "I know Jud," he said slowly. "Jud didn't do it."

Dianne Bryant jumped to her feet and glared at Ho- mer across the room. "Lots of other people know Jud! I know Jud!" she shouted. "Seems as if you have an awful short memory. You were awful mad the night that boy broke all those windows!"

Homer made no reply, but looked at her steadily until she sat down and burst into angry tears.

Captain Ben sighed deeply. That girl would say any- thing, any time, to fight with Homer. She'd stirred up a lot of people, who were nodding their heads as if they agreed with her.

He got to his feet heavily. "I have just one thing more to say," the old man said slowly, looking earnestly from one face to another. "However that fire started,

Jud put it out. He was scared enough for it to come natural to run away and leave it burning. But he stayed right there and fought that fire with his bare hands. Has everyone forgotten that?"

To everyone's surprise, Captain Lu, who took seriously his office as impartial moderator, began to clap. Mrs. Gilley joined him, as did Mr. York. Homer not only clapped hard, but stamped his feet loudly on the floor. Captain Ben didn't clap, but he smiled a little and the weight in his chest lightened.

Suddenly Ladder moved clumsily to the front of the room, a frown on his face. Something had happened that he could not understand. For a while everyone had thought he was a hero. And now, suddenly, they were all clapping for Jud!

"You didn't ask *me*," he said importantly. "I know more'n anyone. I was there first." Ladder was not slouching now. He threw back his shoulders proudly. "No one saw what a good shot I was," he went on. "I shot a hole no bigger than a quarter in the shed window—right over the latch too. Then I hid. No one could see me, but I could see everything."

Ladder looked around the room in a pleased way. Everyone was paying attention to him now. "Jud came up to the big house," he said. "Then he went out to the garage and moved a big pile of brush." He paused. "That would have made an *awful* good fire," he said almost regretfully.

Captain Lu leaned forward. When he spoke it was in a flattering voice. "You know all about the real fire," he said softly. "You're *smart*. What happened next?"

Ladder straightened his shoulders. "Jud saw the hole I made in the window," he said slowly. "He went in and looked around. He lit a lamp. Then he came out and went away." He paused. "I hoped he'd leave the lamp going, but when I went in, it was dark." Then he was silent again.

Captain Lu spoke coaxingly. "But Jud had started the fire, hadn't he, Ladder?" he asked.

Ladder stood even taller and looked around proudly. "He didn't start no fire!" he cried. "That old match I lit broke right in half and fell to the floor. I started the fire, and it was real good at first." Suddenly his face crinkled with fear. "Then it got hot," he said in a scared voice. "I ran. I ran like everything and called the men."

The room was very still. No one moved or whispered.

Captain Lu sighed heavily. "Thank you, Ladder," he said very soberly. "Thank you for telling us just how it happened." He looked around the room, noticing each face—some ashamed; some, like Mrs. Gilley's and Captain Ben's, very happy.

Mr. York rose to his feet. He too looked around. "I'm not a voting member of this town," he said, "but I've learned an important lesson tonight, and I guess I don't need to say what it is. I'm ashamed of anything I said which made anyone doubt Jud, and, because I doubted him a little myself, I'd like to make a motion." He paused and smiled. "I guess as it's not a regular town meeting I can make a motion."

Someone in the back of the room began to clap.

Mr. York held up his hand. "I move," he said, "that we go on record, here and now, that we're grateful to Jud; that we think he did his duty and more than his duty; that we're proud of him."

Then the clapping broke out all over the room.

Captain Ben rubbed his eyes with the back of his hand. "He didn't do anything wrong," he whispered. "I *knew* he didn't do anything wrong!"

12. Maybe—Perhaps—Do
You Suppose?

WHEN Jud awoke, the morning after the meeting at the school house, sunlight was pouring into his room. He propped himself up on one elbow and looked toward the harbor, which was a sparkling blue. The sails of Mr. York's boat were raised, drying out in the fresh, cool wind. He watched the people on the road and saw Mrs. Gilley setting out a pan of milk for her cats at the back of the store. Suddenly he was startled by a voice at the door. He turned and saw Miz Hanks holding a big tray.

"Guess you could do with a real breakfast," she said, and put the tray down on the chest of drawers. She plumped up the pillows and, putting a strong bony arm around him, pulled him up so that he was almost sitting up straight. Jud stared at her. She was being real *nice!* But Miz Hanks wouldn't meet his eyes. She bustled about, pulling up a chair beside the bed. She brought the tray and sat down beside him. She looked quickly at his bandaged hands.

"Don't seem 's if you'd be much good feeding yourself," she commented, and began to uncover the plates of food. There was oatmeal sprinkled liberally with brown sugar and what looked like a good lot of thick yellow cream. There was a good stack of flannel cakes with butter running down the sides and a generous lacing of maple sugar. There was a small glass of fruit juice and a very large glass of foamy milk. Miz Hanks had even brought a plateful of real good scraps for Skipper! It was all too good to be true.

"Now," Miz Hanks said briskly, "what'll you have first?"

That was the beginning of a wonderful day. After the big breakfast, Miz Hanks brought up a bowl of warm water and sponged his face, neck, and shoulders. She got some soap in his eyes and a deal of water on his pajamas, but he felt better for the wash-up. He had a queer feeling all the time that Miz Hanks was trying to tell him something, but she worked in silence and soon went off to do her housework.

Very shortly after that Captain Ben appeared. Without saying anything about the meeting the night before, he lifted a great weight from Jud's mind by saying that Ladder had accidentally started the fire at Mr. York's. "Poor Ladder," the old man said, shaking his head. "He thought he'd done something smart when the fire started. He always liked it when there was something exciting going on in town, and this was exciting, all right. He didn't go to cause any trouble. He's as gentle as a lamb and just about as bright."

A little later the doctor came and changed the dressings on Jud's hands and leg. The burn on his leg looked red and angry, but the pain was almost gone. The clumsy hand bandages were changed to strips of adhesive over gauze, so Jud could use his hands more easily.

During the rest of the day quite a little procession of village people climbed the stairs to see Jud. Mrs. Crockett brought him some books from the Hardwick library. Mrs. Gilley left a big bowl of floating island in the icebox for him before she puffed up the stairs to his room. She even gave the boy a quick motherly hug, which embarrassed him painfully, but he knew it was just Mrs. Gilley's way and accepted it as bravely as possible.

Late in the afternoon Homer came, grinning from ear to ear. He started to clap Jud on the shoulder, but stopped suddenly and patted Skipper instead. "Do you still hurt bad?" he asked anxiously.

Jud shook his head. "I'm kind of stiff and achy. But I feel good. I really feel good. I'll be out of here pretty soon." He paused, looking a little puzzled. "It's not so bad being laid up," he said slowly. "A whole lot of people have been coming to see me, bringing me things, saying they hope I'll get well soon and things like that. Everybody's being real nice, even Miz Hanks. Seems as if they think I'm all right," he concluded.

Homer laughed. "Guess they do," he said in a rough

voice. Then, as if he wanted to change the subject, he said, "'Twon't be any time before you'll be going out to your camp again."

Jud's eyes grew bright. "And maybe I can get that stove. There's one in Mr. York's shed, just the one I'd like. It's the smallest one he has, and maybe he would sell it to me. Would he, do you think, Homer? Would he?"

The young man looked at the boy. Then he stood up. "Tell you what," he said, "I'll go right down there and ask him. I'll tell him you'd like to make him an offer. And I'll come back and let you know what he says." Then he was gone.

Jud lay back on his pillows. "Please," he whispered, "please let Mr. York sell me that little stove!"

When Homer reached Mr. York's place, he found him sitting on the porch, looking out over the blue, white-capped water. Seated on the steps was Father Tom. "Mr. York," Homer said, "I've been up to see Jud."

Mr. York looked alarmed. "He's all right, isn't he?" he asked anxiously. "He's feeling some better?"

"He's a whole lot better," Homer said reassuringly. "He's thinking about getting out to Nubbin again. Guess you know he's built a sort of camp out there. It's pretty small, but it's snug and tight, and he thinks a lot of it."

Mr. York chuckled. "I built a camp when I was his age. Wouldn't have taken a million dollars for it, either."

Homer drew a long breath. "Mr. York," he said earnestly, "there's just one thing in the world that Jud wants more than anything else—he wants a stove for his camp. Just now he told me he saw a real small stove in your shed the day of the fire. He asked me to find out if you'd consider selling it to him."

"*Sell it!*" roared Mr. York. "Why, I'll give it to him! I'd give him anything he wanted. I was trying to think of some kind of reward for what he did—putting out that fire. Sell him that stove? Nonsense!"

Homer sat down on the steps, greatly relieved. He'd had no idea how Mr. York would take his suggestion.

Mr. York got to his feet and pulled some keys out of his pocket. "Let's go find that stove, if you're sure which one it is," he said, and came down the porch steps.

Father Tom spoke quietly. "Mr. York," he said, "could we talk about this a minute?"

Mr. York stopped and stared at the young priest. "What's there to talk about?" he asked almost angrily. "I said I'd give Jud the stove he wants, and I will."

"And that was good of you," Father Tom said. "I'm sure that was the impulse of a kind and generous heart. But I wonder—wouldn't it mean something special to Jud if the stove weren't a reward or any kind of payment, but if he bought it out of the money he's earned?" The young priest hesitated and then went on. "He's tried very hard," he said gently. "He's done his best to be responsible and trustworthy. I don't think I'm saying this very well, but wouldn't it be a kind of reward—a special kind—if he could *buy* that stove?"

Mr. York said nothing for a long moment. He stood looking down at the young man, thinking, remembering a long time ago when he was Jud's age. Then he came down the steps and put his hand on Father Tom's shoulder. "You're right. You're absolutely right," he said. Then he turned to Homer. "Let's go up to see Jud," he said, smiling broadly. "Let's go together and tell him I have a stove, a small stove, just right for a small camp on a small island. Let's tell him I have a stove for sale!"

13. This Way, It's Just Right

ONE DAY late in August the old men on the dock watched with interest as Jud and Homer loaded the dory. First they set amidships, on the floor boards, the small stove Jud had bought from Mr. York. It was clean and shining now, every bit of dirt and rust rubbed away and its brass knobs brightly polished.

Then, while his elderly friends shouted a good deal of quite unnecessary and uncomplimentary advice, Captain Ben stepped into the dory nimbly and settled himself in the stern seat. This brought the bow of the boat way out of the water, so Jud jumped into the bow, followed by Skipper. Homer handed the boy a galvanized pail, which gave forth a tantalizing tinkling sound when it was moved, and then got into the boat himself and put the oars in the oarlocks.

"You'll never make it!" shouted Captain Lu, slapping his knee. "That old feller in the stern is a Jonah, sure as you're born. You'll sink like a plummet, the first wave that hits you."

Captain Ben's only answer was to raise his white cap

in a polite salute and to fix his eyes firmly on the course out through the moorings. Though the boat was heavily loaded, Homer rowed briskly out of the harbor.

"Pull a mite harder on your port oar," the old man ordered mildly.

Homer did so, glancing over his shoulder at Jud, who was smiling broadly. He pointed to the shore. "Don't let them catch us!" the boy cried excitedly.

Down on the dock landing, Homer could see Mr. York and Father Tom. Mr. York was carrying the outboard

motor, and Father Tom was in the dinghy, ready to cast off. Homer rowed even more strongly.

Just as the bow of the dory nudged into the shore of Nubbin, and Jud jumped ashore, the dinghy appeared. Jud showed Mr. York where to tie up and then a little procession went up over the rocks to the camp. Homer carried the stove. Captain Ben carried the stovepipe. Father Tom carried the jangling pail, sloshing the cold sea water in it recklessly. Skipper ran ahead, almost dancing in excitement, scaring away a gathering of

seagulls that had been sunning themselves on the rocks.

Jud ran ahead of the four men. He unlocked the padlock on the door of his camp and pushed up the window to let in sun and air. He had swept out the one small room the day before, and had set down four flat stones for the stove to rest on. His eyes were shining, and his cheeks were red. This was *it!* This was the day he had hardly dared hope for.

All the men had to duck their heads to go in the door, and it was a pretty snug fit when they were all inside the room. To Jud's delight, his placing of the stones needed only one small change, and the little stove sat on them firmly, as if it belonged there—as indeed it did.

Homer had brought his augur and bit, so, when the stove was in place and they had all figured the place where the stovepipe would go through the roof, he drilled a small hole, into which he fitted the blade of Jud's keyhole saw. In less time than it takes to tell it, he had cut a neat round hole, through which they passed the stovepipe. The men looked at it admiringly.

"Do you know what?" said Father Tom. "I think we ought to see if it draws!"

So Jud ran out and gathered a small armful of dry driftwood and twigs. He crumpled a sheet of old newspaper and put it in the firebox, laying the wood on it carefully and being sure to leave space for a draft.

Captain Ben found some big wooden matches in his

pocket. There was a sort of solemn silence while Jud lit a match and touched it to the paper. The bright flame leaped up to lick at the driftwood. In a minute or two there was a lovely crackling noise.

Jud ran out of the camp. "Come out, come out!" he cried. "Come and see the smoke coming out of my chimney."

The four men looked at one another and smiled. Then they went outside. A steady swirl of blue smoke rose briskly on the still air. *It looked just wonderful!*

There had been very little wood in the stove, and the fire died down in a few moments. Jud took the men back into the camp and showed them the bench he had made, and the shelf, where he had put a cup without a handle, a cracked plate, and a bent fork. Hanging on nails behind the shelf was a shiny new frying pan from the dime store in Hardwick.

Captain Ben looked around in a measuring sort of way. "I'd thought," he said, "of building a bunk in your room at home. But we could build one here instead. A *small* bunk," he added. "You'd want to sleep out here some-times, I'd think."

"Oh, I would," Jud agreed. Then he remembered something suddenly. He looked a little embarrassed. "I thought," he said almost shyly, "that as this is your first visit to my camp, we might have some"—he hesitated, and then went on confidently—"some *refreshments*. There's some real good pop in that pail."

He looked around. There was really no way for everyone to sit down in that small room. "It's nice outside on the rocks," he went on. "We'll have our refreshments outside."

The men settled themselves more or less comfortably on the rocks in front of the camp. Jud passed around the pail in which the bottles of orange pop had been kept cold and tingly. Everyone praised Jud's refreshments, and the boy was more and more pleased.

He looked from one man to another. "When I built this place," he said slowly, "I wanted it for a secret, to have all by myself." He thought for a moment. Then he smiled. "It's better this way," he said firmly. "This way, it's *just right!*"

Along the rocky shore of Mr. York's place, Mrs. Gilley and Miz Hanks picked their way slowly. They stood still and looked across the narrow stretch of water between Easterly Point and Nubbin Island. On the rocks nearest to them were the four men, sitting in the sun, drinking pop. Before them stood Jud, Skipper very close to him. The boy's head was held high, and he stood straight and proud.

Miz Hanks stared and then turned to Mrs. Gilley. "That Jud!" she said almost pleasantly.

Mrs. Gilley smiled. She looked at the small head of sun-bleached hair and at the boy's tanned face. "That Jud!" she echoed lovingly.